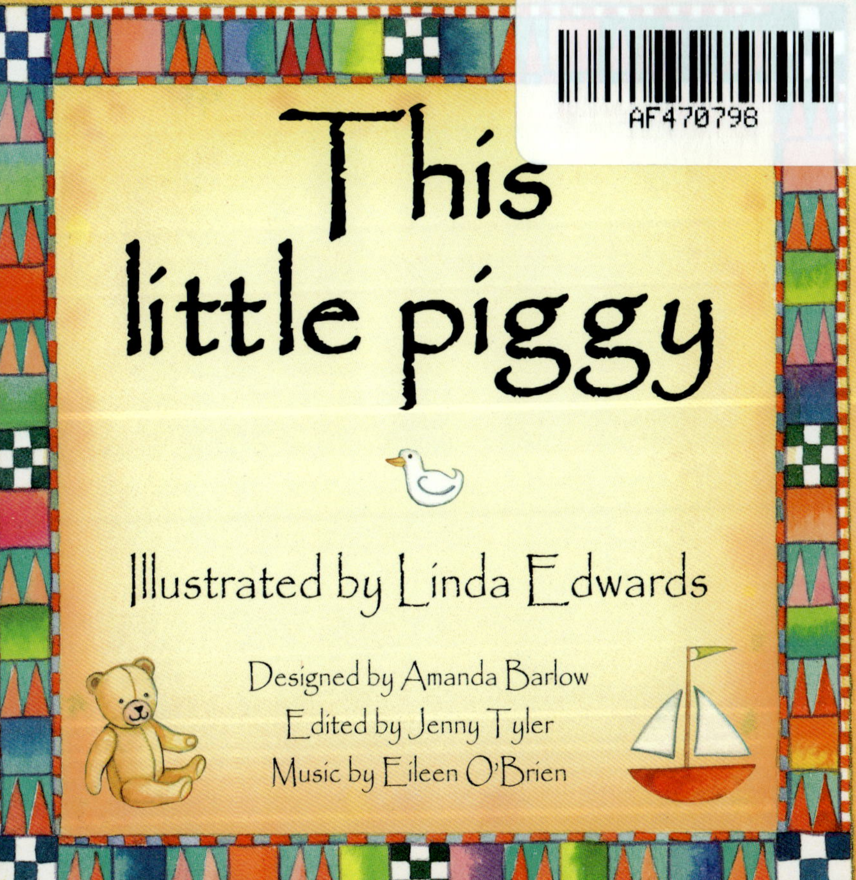

This little piggy

Illustrated by Linda Edwards

Designed by Amanda Barlow
Edited by Jenny Tyler
Music by Eileen O'Brien

This little piggy went to market,

This little piggy
stayed at home,

This little piggy had roast beef,

This little piggy had none,

And this little piggy cried
"Wee, wee, wee"
All the way home.

This lit - tle pig-gy went to mar - ket,
This lit - tle pig - gy stayed at home,
This lit - tle pig - gy had roast beef,

This   lit - tle pig - gy had   none,   And
this   lit - tle pig - gy cried "Wee, wee, wee"
All   the   way   home. _______

Toe rhyme actions

This little piggy went to market,
(Twiddle big toe)
This little piggy stayed at home,
(Twiddle next biggest toe)
This little piggy had roast beef,
(Twiddle middle toe)

This little piggy had none,
(Twiddle next toe)
And this little piggy cried
"Wee, wee, wee" all the way home.
(Twiddle little toe and tickle all the

way up)

First published in 2001 by Usborne Publishing Ltd,
83-85 Saffron Hill, London EC1N 8RT, England. www.usborne.com
Copyright © 2001 Usborne Publishing Ltd. Printed in China.
The name Usborne and the devices ⚓ are Trade marks of Usborne
Publishing Ltd. All rights reserved. No part of this publication may be
reproduced, stored in a retrieval system, or transmitted in any form by any
means, electronic, mechanical, photocopying, recording or otherwise without
the prior permission of the publisher. UE. First published in America in 2002.